Bubba heard a mouse

calling for help

words by Bubba's Dad
illustrated by Faryn Hughes

Illustration by Faryn Hughes
Book design by Kurt Mueller

Library of Congress Control Number: 2016914834
CreateSpace Independent Publishing Platform,
North Charleston, SC

ISBN-13: 978-1537316444
ISBN-10: 1537316443

Dedication

To all of my Facebook friends.
Those who are in this book
and those who are not.

My story is our story.

Special thanks to
Miss Faryn Hughes
and Mr Kurt Mueller
for turning a simple story
into a thing of beauty.

And to my mom.

Because she never
lets me forget how much
she loves me.

Bubba

Chapter 1

Bubba had very big ears that never slept.
Even late at night his ears stayed wide awake.

Listening. Listening very carefully.
To every sound in the house.

One day just before dawn, Bubba was
sleeping in the big bed, snuggled in tightly
between Mom and Dad.

He was dreaming and his stubby Bubba tail
was wagging in his sleep.

But he was still listening,
listening very carefully.

And that's when he heard a SNAP!

Bubba's stubby tail stopped wagging.
He opened one eye.

"What was that?" he wondered.

Bubba listened VERY carefully.

All was quiet.

Bubba tried to go back to sleep. But he couldn't.

All he could do was listen, listen very carefully.

And then he heard something he'd never heard before.

A tiny little voice drifted into the room.

Mom didn't hear it. Dad didn't hear it.

But Bubba's very big ears heard it quite clearly.

Bubba's eyes opened wide. And his head tilted
this way and that.

He listened, and listened, and listened some more.
Yes, he was sure.

Bubba heard a little voice. And it was calling for help!

At that moment he knew what he had to do.

So he unsnuggled himself from between
Mom and Dad.

Then he tip, tip, tiptoed down the little steps
next to the big bed.

Like a white shadow he slid silently out
of the bedroom.

Off he raced down the hall, through the dining room
and across the kitchen floor.

Bubba zoomed down the basement stairs …

And into the family room …

Where he came to a sliding stop in front of the toy box
where his monkey toys slept.

One by one, the monkey toys peeked over the edge
of the toy box and saw Bubba standing there listening.
Listening very carefully.

Rubbing their eyes, the monkey toys whispered
to Bubba.

"Bubba!" they said, "What do you hear?"

"Is it an alien?"

"Shhhh!" Bubba said. "It's not an alien.
Someone needs help."

Bubba tiptoed very quietly to the laundry room door
and pushed it open with his flat French Bulldog nose.

One of Bubba's monkey toys whispered, "Bubba,
you're not allowed in there."

"Bubba, you'll get in trouble, BIG trouble," the other
monkey whispered, and stuck out his tongue.

Bubba looked over his shoulder back
at the monkey toys.

He thought, and then he thought some more.

"I have to go in," he said. "Someone needs me."

Bubba gingerly put one paw in the laundry room.

And then another. And another. And another.

He crept slowly past the laundry room sink
where he got his baths.

And the clothes dryer that went thump, thump,
thump.

He looked up at the small window high on the wall.

The alien who lived next door was peeking
in the window and watching something very closely.

Bubba followed the alien's gaze to the old refrigerator
in the corner.

One more time, Bubba listened,
listened very carefully.

Then he heard it. He heard that little voice again.

"Help me," it called. "Somebody please help me!"

"Somebody? Anybody?"

"Can you hear me?" the little voice asked.

Bubba cautiously peeked around the side of the fridge
back into a dark, musty corner where no doggy
had ever peeked.

He saw something that nearly broke his Bubba heart.

A mouse. A tiny little mouse with very big ears
just like his own.

The sad little thing looked up at him
with tears in her eyes.

Bubba was a very careful dog. So he slowly
put his flat Frenchie nose down to sniff.

Sniff, sniff.

"Little Mouse, what's wrong?" he asked.

With a trembling voice Little Mouse said,
"My tail is caught in this trap. And I can't move.
And it hurts real bad."

Bubba sniffed the rusty old mouse trap.

It smelled a hundred years old. It smelled mean.

The fur on the back of Bubba's neck stood up.

Little Mouse wiped her eyes with the back of her tiny mouse hand.

"What's your name?" she asked. "Can you help me?"

Bubba backed up just a bit and looked down at Little Mouse.

"My name is Bubba and I will do my best."

Chapter 2

Bubba sniffed the trap again. He could see the problem.

Bubba said, "Hold onto my ear. Hold onto it tight."

"I will try to pull you free."

Little Mouse grabbed one of Bubba's big ears with her two tiny little mouse hands and held on tight.

Bubba put one paw on the trap and very carefully began to pull.

"Ouch, ouch, ouch!" Little Mouse cried.

Bubba jumped back at the very first "ouch!"

"I'm sorry Little Mouse," Bubba said. "Did I hurt you?"

"No Bubba, I think I'm okay," the mouse said.

"Try again. You must try again."

So Bubba pulled again, a little harder this time.

Little Mouse gritted her teeth and held onto Bubba's ear with all her strength.

Little Mouse tried not to cry but the trap
was so mean. So very mean.

"Ouch, Bubba, ouch!" she cried.

Bubba stopped pulling. He couldn't stand the sound
of anyone or anything in pain – not even a mouse.

He lay down in front of his new friend. The wrinkles
on his forehead were more wrinkly than usual.

"What are we going to do, Little Mouse?"

"The trap is strong. And I'm afraid. I'm afraid I will
hurt you."

Little Mouse looked down at her tail caught
in the trap.

Then she looked up at Bubba and his very big ears.

"Listen Bubba, listen very carefully."

"We need somebody to help us."

"Somebody who's not afraid."

Her little eyes narrowed and she made her
tiny little hands into two tiny little fists.

"Somebody who's not afraid of ANYTHING!"

Bubba's eyes lit up. "I know who can help us," he said.

Then he picked up Little Mouse in his mouth,
trap and all, and raced out of the laundry room.

He ran past the monkey toys who hooted
and hollered, and jumped up and down
in the toy box.

Bubba raced up the basement stairs and out
the doggy door into the cool, crisp early morning air.

He flew like an arrow across the backyard,
under the fence and down the street
to find his fearless friends.

Chapter 3

Mojo, Ocho and Herman were three fearless little Frenchies who lived on the next block.

The sun had just come up but they were already out bouncing from one trampoline to the next between their backyards.

Back and forth over the fence they flew.
First Mojo. Then Ocho. Then Herman.

Doing somersaults and cartwheels in the air.

Bubba's head went back and forth, back and forth, watching them fly.

He set Little Mouse at his feet and called to his friends.

"Help! Down here! I need your help," Bubba barked.

Boing! Boing! Boing! One by one the three flying Frenchies landed in a circle around Bubba and Little Mouse.

"This little mouse is stuck and I'm not brave enough to free her myself," said Bubba.

Herman, Mojo and Ocho crowded around.

"I'm brave enough!" barked Herman.

"I'm fearless!" shouted Mojo.

"Bring it on!" said Ocho.

Herman shoved Mojo out of the way, "I'm braver than you, Mojo!"

Mojo shoved Herman back. "No way! NOTHING scares me!"

Ocho sized up the situation and said "I'll hold the trap . . ."

Herman chimed in, "And I'll grab her feet . . ."

Mojo shouted, "And I'll hold her arms. . ."

"And we'll jump up and down on the trampoline until she is FREE!" barked Ocho.

"Stop!" Little Mouse shouted.

"What you want to do is not wise. Not wise at all!"

Mojo and Herman and Ocho sat back,
surprised at the big voice from the little mouse.

Little Mouse looked up at Bubba and his very big ears.

"Listen Bubba, listen very carefully."

"We need somebody to help us.
Somebody who's fearless but gentle, too."

Bubba sighed. He thought for a moment and said,
"I know who can help us. I have two friends who
are very kind, very gentle."

So he picked up Little Mouse, trap and all,
and ran down the sidewalk in search of his kind
and gentle friends.

Chapter 4

Gatsby was sitting on the porch swing, holding paws with his girlfriend Bella.

Bubba watched the swing go back and forth, back and forth.

"Gatsby! Bella!" he said. "Can you help my little friend?"

They hopped down from the swing and carefully sniffed Little Mouse.

Their soft Frenchie snorts tickled Little Mouse's ears. She rubbed them and smiled.

Their gentleness made her feel safe. And her tail didn't hurt quite so bad when she looked up into their kind eyes.

"Hello, Mr. Gatsby. Hello Miss Bella," smiled Little Mouse.

She reached out her little mouse hand to shake Bella's paw when she suddenly felt faint.

The whole world felt like it was spinning and she quickly sat down to catch her breath.

Bella stroked the little mouse's forehead with her paw.

"Your friend is very weak Bubba. When did she last eat?" asked Bella, her voice filled with concern.

Gatsby looked at Little Mouse very closely through his big round spectacles.

"*Fromage*," Gatsby said in French. "She needs cheese, Bubba, this mouse needs cheese."

Bubba shook his head in disbelief. "Where am I going to get cheese?"

"I'm not allowed to eat human food. I'm only allowed to eat my special Bubba kibble!"

Bella and Gatsby looked at each other and both barked out the same name at the same time.

"SHORTY!"

"Shorty has human food!" said Gatsby.

"LOTS of human food!" said Bella.

Bubba's eyes lit up. "*Merci,* Gatsby and thank you, Bella!"

And then he picked up Little Mouse and off he ran to find his friend Shorty.

Chapter 5

Bubba stuck his head into Shorty's doggy door and barked.

"Shorty are you home?"

Shorty barked back in his big, booming Pit Bull voice.

"Bubba! I'm in here, little bro!"

Bubba trotted through the house and into the kitchen where Shorty was making breakfast. His third one of the morning.

"Bubba! How many bacon pancakes do you want?" Shorty asked, flipping a pancake high in the air and catching it in his big Pit Bull mouth.

"None for me, Shorty. I need some cheese for my little friend. She's hungry and needs our help."

Chewing with his mouth full, Shorty leaned down and sniffed the little mouse at his feet.

Sniff, sniff.

Little Mouse crinkled her nose and sniffed him back.

"Hello, Mr. Shorty. You smell like bacon," she said.

"Why thank you, Little Mouse. It's my bacon aftershave!"

"Would you like some bacon?" Shorty asked.

He opened the refrigerator door with his nose, "I have bacon pancakes, bacon omelets, bacon-flavored orange juice and bacon-flavored bacon."

"We just need a little piece of cheese," said Bubba.

Shorty dug deep into the fridge and pulled out a small yellow wedge of cheese and crumbled it up between his paws.

"Here we go, Bacon Cheddar!"

Little Mouse took a piece of cheese in her little mouse hands and quickly nibbled it down.

"Mmm, thank you Mr. Shorty. This is wonderful. May I have another piece?"

While Little Mouse nibbled the cheese,
the pink color returned to her ears and she started
to feel much, much better.

"Thanks Shorty, we have to go," Bubba said.

"Any time, Brotha!" Shorty called after Bubba
as he headed for the door.

"Sure you don't want a bacon pancake
for the road?"

Chapter 6

Back out on the sidewalk Bubba stopped to think.

"Little Mouse," he said, "we need to figure out a way to get you out of this trap."

"But how?" Little Mouse asked.

"None of your friends have thumbs. And that makes it impossible for them to get my tail out of this rusty old thing."

"I can solve that problem," a smooth, silky voice purred.

The fur on the back of Bubba's neck stood straight up. He did a 180-degree Frenchie spin to face the source of the purring voice.

It was the alien that lived next door to Bubba.

The one with the coal black fur and glowing eyes.

The one that peeked in his basement window at night.

And hissed at him when he went for his walk in the morning.

(Bubba believed that all cats are aliens from another planet. And this alien was as alien as an alien can get!)

Bubba covered Little Mouse with his paw
to keep her from harm.

"Go away, alien. There's nothing you can do to help."

Little Mouse looked up at the smiling alien
and hid her face behind her little mouse hands.

"But there is. Look Bubba. Look at my paw. I have
something here that can solve the problem."

The alien slowly turned over his paw. Bubba looked
more closely. Out of the tip of the first toe popped
a long, sharp, alien claw.

"See that? I can use that to lift the bar that has trapped
your little friend's tail."

Then the alien slowly turned over his other paw
from which two more claws popped out.

"And then with this paw I will gently lift your friend
out of the trap and hand her back to you,"
purred the alien's soft, velvety voice.

Bubba looked at the alien's friendly grin.

"I don't know …" he hesitated.

Then Bubba looked deep into the alien's eyes.
They were very bright and they glowed
and twinkled in the light.

"I guess it's worth a try," said Bubba.
"You promise to give her right back?"

"Oh yes," purred the alien, "I promise."

Bubba cupped Little Mouse in his paws
and slowly began to hand her to the alien.

At that moment, another voice rang out …

"EVIL DOER, STOP!"

Bubba blinked twice, shook his head, and quickly pulled Little Mouse away from the alien's grasp.

The alien hissed super loud. And Bubba spun around.

It was Ace, the crime fighting Frenchie
– out on neighborhood patrol.

"Planet Hairball called, it's time to go home!"
growled the caped canine.

The alien hissed again and took a step forward.

Ace dropped into a Ninja crouch
with his gloved paws ready for action.

The alien stopped in his tracks and glared at Ace
with its glowing eyes.

"Bubba, listen," said Ace. "Listen very carefully.
This one is playing mind tricks. Go to the Big River.
Find the Wise One. She will tell you what to do."

Little Mouse whispered to Bubba, "Run, Bubba, run!"

Bubba knew Ace could take care of himself.

So he grabbed Little Mouse and ran.
And didn't look back.

Chapter 7

Bubba and Little Mouse stood at the edge of the Big River.

The Wise One lived in a tiny house farther down the river and Bubba had no way to get his little friend there.

When Bubba was a puppy he was afraid of puddles. So now when he went to the beach to play he didn't like to go in the water too deep.

"What do we do, Bubba?" asked Little Mouse.

Before he could answer, Bubba saw something that made his stubby Bubba tail wag super-fast.

It was a bright pink surfboard with a cute Frenchie surfer girl riding a whitewater wave!

"Cherie! Is that you?" he called.

"Bubba is that you?" Cherie the Surf Dog called back.

Bubba couldn't believe his luck.

Cherie was on vacation in Minnesota from California. And she brought her surfboard, too! What were the chances?

"Cherie! Can you give us a ride to BeTti's house?"

"Hop on, let's go!"

Bubba whispered to Little Mouse, "Hold on tight to me and I will hold on tight to Cherie's life jacket. She's an expert. We will be safe."

And so off they went, surfing this way and that down the Big River, Bubba hanging onto Cherie's life jacket for dear life and Little Mouse hanging on even tighter.

When they splashed ashore at BeTti's house, Bubba gave Cherie the high paw.

"You rock, Surfer Girl!"

"Thanks dude," Cherie said. "You're pretty gnarly yourself."

"I'll wait for you," she smiled. "We can paddle back together!"

Chapter 8

BeTti with a capital "T" was a very beautiful, very wise Boston Terrier.

She was much smaller than Bubba, with a bright, colorful green dress and a sparkling diamond collar. Her eyes were jet black and very, very big.

Bubba thought she looked like a magical fairy princess.

"Bubba! What happened to your friend?" BeTti asked, gently nuzzling Little Mouse with her nose.

"BeTti this is Little Mouse. She is caught in a trap, but I am not brave enough or wise enough to free her myself."

Bubba sighed. "What should I do?"

Little Mouse held one of BeTti's delicate little paws in her own tiny mouse hands.

"Please, Miss Princess BeTti," said Little Mouse. "I am afraid. WE are afraid. Can you help Bubba decide the best thing to do?"

BeTti gently squeezed Little Mouse's hands.

"There's only one thing to do, Little Mouse."

Then BeTti looked at Bubba and said, "Listen, listen very carefully, Bubba."

"Who is wise, and kind, and careful? Who can you trust to help you when no one else can?"

"Who loves you more than ANYTHING in the world?"

Bubba thought for a moment.

"More than anything?"

A look of understanding came over Bubba's face.

"My mom and dad," said Bubba looking down at Little Mouse.

"I can trust my mom and dad. They will know what to do."

Bubba gave BeTti a quick Bubba smooch on the cheek.

"THANKS BeTti! You're the best BFF EVER!"

Chapter 9

Mom and Dad were just waking up as Bubba burst into the room.

Mom sat up on the edge of the bed, stretched out her arms and looked down at Bubba.

She yawned and said, "Good morning, Bubba. What do you have in your mouth?"

Bubba's stubby tail wagged the way it always did when he heard his mom's voice.

He set the trap down at his mom's feet and wagged his stubby tail a little faster.

He was very pleased that he finally had someone who could help his little friend.

Bubba looked up at Mom. Little Mouse looked up at Mom. Mom looked down at Little Mouse and . . .

SCREEEEEEEEEEEEEEEAMED!

"A mouse, a mouse, Bubba's got a mouse!!!" Mom screamed at the top of her lungs.

Bubba's dad jumped straight up out of bed so high that his head hit the ceiling.

"What? Where? What?" Dad shouted, rubbing his head.

Standing on top of the bed, Bubba's mom poked her finger over and over at Bubba.

"Down there! Bubba's got a mouse!" she shouted frantically.

"Do something! Do something! Do something!"

Bubba looked up at his mom. He tilted his head one way and then the other.

"Why is she pointing and shouting?" he thought.

Bubba looked down at Little Mouse. And back up
at his mom pointing at him. He tilted his head.
Trying to understand.

He watched as his dad snuck around the side of the
bed with a wastebasket clutched tightly in both hands.

Bubba tilted his head at his dad, too.

Then it came to him. His mom and dad were afraid.
Afraid of a little mouse.

Somehow, someway, he had to explain to them
that there was nothing to be afraid of.

So Bubba curled up around Little Mouse
and put his head on the floor. He closed his eyes
and became very quiet.

"Listen, Mom and Dad, listen very carefully,"
Bubba thought to himself.

"I know you're afraid. But my friend needs our help."

Dad moved closer. The wastebasket in his hands hovered over Bubba and Little Mouse.

"We have to be brave," thought Bubba. "We are her only hope."

Bubba's mom stopped pointing and her voice grew very soft.

"Wait," said Bubba's mom. "Bubba's trying to tell us something."

Bubba let out a sigh. Little Mouse did, too.

"Look, the mouse is in a trap," Mom said, getting off the bed.

"Bubba didn't CATCH a mouse," Mom said.

"Bubba is trying to SAVE a mouse," Dad said.

That's when something wonderful happened. Bubba's mom and dad knelt down on the floor next to him and Little Mouse.

"Do you need some help, little guy?" Bubba's dad asked him, setting the wastebasket aside.

Bubba looked down at Little Mouse and back up at his dad. He wagged his stubby tail back and forth, around and around.

"Yes, I do," thought Bubba.

Mom gently stroked his ears and said, "You can trust us, Bubba. We will help you."

And then, even though Mom was still kind of scared, she held the trap so Bubba's dad could use his strong dad fingers and thumbs to slowly lift the rusty metal bar.

Little Mouse held onto one of Bubba's very big ears with both little hands. She kept her eyes closed tightly and said a tiny little mouse prayer.

Bubba listened very carefully.

When he heard the rusty old trap squeeeeek open, he gently raised his head with Little Mouse still holding on tightly to his ear.

And she was free at last.

Chapter 10

That afternoon, Bubba threw a pawty at the Bubba bungalow to celebrate Little Mouse's freedom.
And everybody had a blast!

Shorty was there grilling bacon cheeseburgers.

"Great job, Brotha!" said Shorty. "That was hard work saving that mouse. I could eat a horse! If it was made out of bacon."

"Let's do ZOOMIES!" barked Herman who zoomed around and around the yard with Ocho and Mojo hot on his tail.

Gatsby and Bella held paws and strolled through Mom's garden admiring her flowers.

Ace showed Princess BeTti some Ninja crime fighter moves.

Cherie worked on her tan.

And the monkey toys entertained themselves by throwing banana peels at the alien on the other side of the fence.

Bubba and Little Mouse sat on the patio, enjoying the warm sunshine and watching their friends have fun.

"Thanks for coming to my rescue, Bubba," she said.

"You're welcome, Little Mouse," said Bubba.

Then the little mouse climbed up onto Bubba's head and gave his big Bubba ear a great big hug.

"You're my hero," she said.

Bubba's ears turned pink. And his stubby Bubba tail wagged super fast.

Chapter 10½

Late that night, dog-tired after a very long day,
Bubba tiptoed up the little steps to the big bed.

He snuggled in tightly between his mom and dad.
Closed his eyes. And let out a big Bubba sigh.

Then he drifted off into a very deep sleep.

But even as he snored, a soft Frenchie snore,
Bubba's very big ears stayed wide awake.

Listening. Listening very carefully.

To every sound in the house.

That is all.

Bubba's Dad

is a writer of children's books and many
other things with words in them. He lives
with Bubba and Bubba's mom in Minnesota
and in California sometimes, too.
He has his own name but most people
just call him Bubba's Dad.

Faryn Hughes

is an illustrator of utopian
and whimsical water-medium works,
imaginative storybook designs for children,
and folklore inspired scenes.
She is also a cat mom of two aliens,
Cash and Finnegan,
who she adores.

Friend Bubba on Facebook!

Bubba calls his book a Facebook fairy tale,
because all of the characters are based on his
real life doggy Facebook friends!

You can friend Bubba,
meet the real dogs behind the story,
and lots more on Facebook
@ Bubba Louie Book Page

You Can Come to the Rescue, Too!

It feels good to come to the rescue
of an animal in need. Please give generously to
your favorite animal rescue organization. Two
of Bubba's favorites are:

French Bulldog Rescue Network
FBRN is an all-volunteer network dedicated to
rescuing, rehabilitating and re-homing French
Bulldogs that have nowhere to go.
www.frenchbulldogrescue.org

S.N.O.R.T.
Short Noses Only Rescue Team
SNORT's mission is to rescue short-nose dogs
(Frenchies, Boston Terriers, Pugs,
English Bulldogs and short-nose mixes).
www.snortrescue.org

Did you like my book?

Give Me a Good Review!
If you liked my book please leave a good review
on Amazon or wherever you bought my book.
I can't wait to read your comments!
Thank you for your support,

Bubba

36636799R00035

Made in the USA
Middletown, DE
07 November 2016